What Kids Say About
Carole Marsh Mysteries . . .

I love the real locations! Reading the book always makes me want to go and visit them all on our next family vacation. My Mom says maybe, but I can't wait!

One day, I want to be a real kid in one of Ms. Marsh's mystery books. I think it would be fun, and I think I am a real character anyway. I filled out the application and sent it in and am keeping my fingers crossed!

History was not my favorite subject till I starting reading Carole Marsh Mysteries. Ms. Marsh really brings history to life. Also, she leaves room for the scary and fun.

I think Christina is so smart and brave. She is lucky to be in the mystery books because she gets to go to a lot of places. I always wonder just how much of the book is true and what is made up. Trying to figure that out is fun!

Grant is cool and funny! He makes me laugh a lot!!

I like that there are boys and girls in the story of different ages. Some mysteries I outgrow, but I can always find a favorite character to identify with in these books.

They are scary, but not too scary. They are funny. I learn a lot. There is always food which makes me hungry. I feel like I am there.

What Parents and Teachers Say About Carole Marsh Mysteries . . .

I think kids love these books because they have such a wealth of detail. I know I learn a lot reading them! It's an engaging way to look at the history of any place or event. I always say I'm only going to read one chapter to the kids, but that never happens—it's always two or three, at least!
—Librarian

Reading the mystery and going on the field trip—Scavenger Hunt in hand—was the most fun our class ever had! It really brought the place and its history to life. They loved the real kids characters and all the humor. I loved seeing them learn that reading is an experience to enjoy!
—4th grade teacher

Carole Marsh is really on to something with these unique mysteries. They are so clever; kids want to read them all. The Teacher's Guides are chock full of activities, recipes, and additional fascinating information. My kids thought I was an expert on the subject—and with this tool, I felt like it!
—3rd grade teacher

My students loved writing their own Real Kids/Real Places mystery book! Ms. Marsh's reproducible guidelines are a real jewel. They learned about copyright and more & ended up with their own book they were so proud of!
—Reading/Writing Teacher

"The kids seem very realistic—my children seemed to relate to the characters. Also, it is educational by expanding their knowledge about the famous places in the books."

"They are what children like: mysteries and adventures with children they can relate to."

"Encourages reading for pleasure."

"This series is great. It can be used for reluctant readers, and as a history supplement."

The Mystery in the

Amazon Rainforest

South America

by Carole Marsh

Copyright ©2007 Carole Marsh/ Gallopade International
All rights reserved.
First Edition

Carole Marsh Mysteries™ and its skull colophon are the property of
Carole Marsh and Gallopade International.

Published by Gallopade International/Carole Marsh Books. Printed in the
United States of America.

Managing Editor: Sherry Moss
Senior Editor: Janice Baker
Assistant Editor: Fran Kramer
Cover Design: Vicki DeJoy
Illlustrations: Yvonne Ford

Picture Credits:

The publisher would like to thank the following for their kind permission to
reproduce the cover photographs.

Matt Ireland, Christopher Waters, Lisa F. Young, R. Fox, © **Images from BigStock
Photo.com**

Gallopade International is introducing SAT words that kids need to
know in each new book we publish. The SAT words are bold in the
story. Look for this special logo beside each word in the glossary.
Happy Learning!

Gallopade is proud to be a member and supporter of these
educational organizations and associations:

American Booksellers Association

American Library Association

International Reading Association

National Association for Gifted Children

The National School Supply and Equipment Association

The National Council for the Social Studies

Museum Store Association

Association of Partners for Public Lands

20 Years Ago . . .

As a mother and an author, one of the fondest periods of my life was when I decided to write mystery books for children. At this time (1979) kids were pretty much glued to the TV, something parents and teachers complained about the way they do about web surfing and blogging today.

I decided to set each mystery in a real place—a place kids could go and visit for themselves after reading the book. And I also used real children as characters. Usually a couple of my own children served as characters, and I had no trouble recruiting kids from the book's location to also be characters.

Also, I wanted all the kids—boys and girls of all ages—to participate in solving the mystery. And, I wanted kids to learn something as they read. Something about the history of the location. And I wanted the stories to be funny. That formula of real+scary+smart+fun served me well.

I love getting letters from teachers and parents who say they read the book with their class or child, then visited the historic site and saw all the places in the mystery for themselves. What's so great about that? What's great is that you and your children have an experience that bonds you together forever. Something you shared. Something you both cared about at the time. Something that crossed all age levels—a good story, a good scare, a good laugh!

20 years later,

Carole Marsh

Hey, kids! As you see—here we are ready to embark on another of our exciting Carole Marsh Mystery adventures! You know, in "real life," I keep very close tabs on Christina, Grant, and their friends when we travel. However, in the mystery books, they always seem to slip away from Papa and me so that they can try to solve the mystery on their own!

I hope you will go to www.carolemarshmysteries.com and apply to be a character in a future mystery book! Well, the *Mystery Girl* is all tuned up and ready for "take-off!"

Gotta go... Papa says so! Wonder what I've forgotten this time?

Happy "Armchair Travel" Reading,

Mimi

About the Characters

Christina, age 10: Mysterious things really do happen to her! Hobbies: soccer, Girl Scouts, anything crafty, hanging out with Mimi, and going on new adventures.

Grant, age 7: Always manages to fall off boats, back into cactuses, and find strange clues—even in real life! Hobbies: camping, baseball, computer games, math, and hanging out with Papa.

Mimi is Carole Marsh, children's book author and creator of Carole Marsh Mysteries, Around the World in 80 Mysteries, Three Amigos Mysteries, Baby's First Mysteries, and many others.

Papa is Bob Longmeyer, the author's real-life husband, who really does wear a tuxedo, cowboy boots and hat, fly an airplane, captain a boat, speak in a booming voice, and laugh a lot!

Travel around the world with Christina and Grant as they visit famous places in 80 countries, and experience the mysterious happenings that always seem to follow them!

Books in
This Series

Table of Contents

Sneaky Snakes

The 30-foot anaconda wrapped itself around Christina's legs. It curled higher and higher—SQUEEZING. *Can't breathe...can't breathe...* She frantically clawed at the air and unknowingly gripped her seven-year-old brother, Grant, around his wrist.

Grant gave her a slight shove in the shoulder and rubbed his arm. "Hey, what gives?"

"Yikes!" Startled awake by her brother, ten-year-old Christina inhaled deeply, and sank back against her airplane seat. "Thank goodness—it was only a dream!" she said. She curled her legs and bent forward to make sure there was really no snake under her seat. Satisfied she had nothing to fear, Christina reached over and patted her brother's sore arm.

"Sorry, Grant," she said. "It must have been all those wild stories Sam told us about the Amazon River and the rainforest."

Sam smiled. Her real name was Samantha, but all her friends called her Sam for short. She sat in the seat next to the window reading one of her many books about the rainforest. She was thrilled to be traveling with Christina, Grant, and their grandparents, Mimi and Papa.

Sam's parents owned a teacher store where she spent much of her time helping her mom after school. Her relationship with Christina and Grant had grown rapidly since the beginning of the school year. She was the same age as Christina, so they hung out a lot together. With so much information at her fingertips, she'd become an avid reader, like her new friends already were. Sam's passion about the destruction of the rainforest had sparked an interest in Mimi, and so off they went on a great new adventure!

Sam knew that Mimi was a famous mystery writer, who traveled around the world to research her latest book. She usually flew with Papa in his little red and white plane, the *Mystery Girl*. Often, like now, Christina and Grant were invited to go along, where they explored new places while the adults did research. The kids always seemed to get involved in a mystery when they traveled, and Sam hoped she could help solve a mystery, too!

The group had changed planes in Miami, Florida, leaving the *Mystery Girl* behind in a special hangar until their return. Papa had personally secured her, and affectionately patted the plane on the nose as he said good-bye.

The long flight to Brazil took about eight hours, so the kids had to find ways to pass the time. The girls absorbed themselves in reading books about the rainforest while Grant napped in the seat next to Christina.

Christina pointed out a picture to Sam. "Look at this!" she said. It was a dazzling, greenish-blue dragonfly resting on a beautiful pink orchid. "The book says that it has a seven-inch wingspan, and can detect movement from as far as 40 feet away. That must make the mosquitoes run for cover!" she said with a chuckle.

Sam laughed, too. "It serves them right for going around sucking everybody's blood."

"Are we there yet?" Grant rubbed his eyes and yawned.

Papa was still snoring softly with his cowboy hat low over his eyes. Mimi didn't want to disturb him, so she turned carefully in her seat, and rested her chin on crossed arms. "Not yet, sleepyhead," she said. She leaned over and gently tapped Christina on her head. "Hey," she said quietly. "What's got you so preoccupied?"

Christina looked up and smiled. "It's a book about the rainforest," she said. Christina was excited to share all that she had learned with Mimi. "It says here, 'The rainforests circle our planet like a beautiful green belt worn by Mother Earth. Each of the millions of animals and plants that makes its home in these jungles is like a jewel, making the belt all the more valuable.' Is that cool or what?"

"Well, I'm impressed," Mimi said. "Not only by that beautiful passage you just read, but by the fact that you're learning why it's so important to preserve our rainforests."

"I never realized how important until I started reading these books," Christina said. "I've learned a lot of amazing facts." She pointed to a page. "Did you know that the Amazon

Rainforest is thought to be the oldest tropical forest area in the world, and may be 100 million years old?"

Mimi smiled. "See? I'm learning something new, too," she replied. "I hadn't realized that the Amazon Rainforest was that old. But because it is so old, I think we take it for granted that it will always be here. That's why I'm writing a book— so that people will begin to notice that things are changing, before it's too late to do anything about it."

Christina frowned. "Someday I'm going to do something special to help save the rainforest," she announced.

Soon they were flying over the Amazon River, and the lush greenery of the rainforest burst into view. In a few minutes they would land at Guarulhos International Airport.

Sam read more tidbits of information aloud from her treasured book. "It says here that the Amazon River basin is largest basin in the world."

"Basin, what's that? Like a sink?" Grant asked.

"Sort of," said Sam. "It's a deep valley where the Amazon River drains, and is surrounded by seven countries." She held up her hand and counted on her fingers: "Colombia, Ecuador, Peru, Bolivia, Venezuela, and Paraguay. Oh, and Brazil, where most of the Amazon River lies—and where we're going," she explained.

"Jeez, you're really smart," Grant said.

Sam smiled at him. "That's because I read all the time."

Christina looked up from her book. "Here's something that should interest you, Grant," she said. "Brazil contains the world's largest rainforest, and thousands of different kinds of insects live there!"

"Tons of bugs! Yippee!" Grant cried. He clapped his hands and bounced up and down in his seat. "Now I'm really excited about seeing the rainforest!"

"Blah!" Christina crossed her eyes at him. She could never figure out Grant's infatuation with creepy, crawly insects. She went back to reading. "Oh, look here. The book also says there's a local legend about the Lost Treasure of the Rainforest."

Grant's head snapped up. "Treasure?" he asked, and rubbed his hands together in glee. "Sounds like the beginning of another cool mystery to me."

"Now don't start, Grant," Mimi said as she turned around in her seat and wagged her finger at him. "We're here on vacation to take in the local sights and sounds while I research my book. And YOU, young man, will try to stay out of trouble this time." She met his blue-eyed gaze with her own and gave him "the look."

Christina glanced up from her book. "Well, that should be a full-time job," she said with a chuckle.

They all laughed at that, and when the FASTEN SEATBELTS sign flashed, Christina, Sam, and Grant strapped in as they prepared to land.

One dreamed of treasure.
One dreamed of mystery.
One dreamed of bugs!

Trailing a
Treasure Map

The plane landed smoothly and taxied to the gate. Everyone was impatient to disembark and stood up as soon as the plane stopped. Passengers hurriedly opened the overhead compartments and grabbed their belongings.

Because there were five people in their group, Papa had instructed everyone to stay in their seats and let the other passengers deplane first.

Grant heard the chime of many cell phones coming to life as the outside door finally opened. Grant people-watched as the passengers quickly filed past him. A wild-haired mother lugged her wailing baby down the aisle. The mother looked like she might cry herself. A young boy was hustled up the aisle by his mother. When she told him to "Move it!" his response  was a loud **POP!** of his bubble gum.

A man wearing a tan Panama hat caught Grant's eye as he trudged up the aisle. A long, jagged scar zigzagged across his left cheek. He juggled several long, white, plastic cylinders under his arm, like those an architect would use to carry drawings. A dark blue laptop computer bag hung over his shoulder. A pair of binoculars and a camera dangled around his neck.

The man in the Panama hat was clearly over-burdened and in a big hurry. He bumped against the seat in front of Grant, and one of the cylinders swung within inches of his nose.

"Hey!" Grant yelled. He pushed the tube away from his face.

The man turned sharply and shot a piercing glance in Grant's direction through wire spectacles, but said nothing. As he hurried on ahead, the cap on one of the cylinders popped off and a scroll of paper slid out. Grant turned his head and watched it roll back under several seats.

"Hey, Mister!" Grant waved his arms and called out. But with all the noise, and the infant still crying, it was hopeless to try to get his attention. Grant tried to run after him, but Papa held his arm out, blocking him in. "Stay in your seat, Grant," he ordered.

"But Papa..." Grant protested.

"Shhh..." Papa put his finger to his lips. "A moment of silence, please. The noise on this plane has been deafening, and my head hurts."

Grant sat quietly, and tried to be patient until the last of the passengers deplaned. Finally, it was their turn. He strapped on his backpack and scrambled out of his seat to follow Mimi and Papa.

Seeing his chance to find the paper, Grant crawled along the floor. He ducked his head under every row of seats down the aisle. Finally, he spotted it, but the paper was wedged under the seat nearest the window. Grant had to really stretch to pull it free. "Whew!" he said. "I got it!"

As Grant pushed himself from under the seat, he felt something gooey on his hand. Stuck to his palm was a wrinkled candy wrapper oozing with melted chocolate and peanut crumbs. "Yuck!" he said to himself.

Grant flung the wrapper aside and wiped his sticky hand down his pants. He carefully unrolled the paper on the seat and tried to smooth it out. It was a map! But a map to where? Grant turned it this way and that way to determine which end was up. When he finally figured it out, he saw a building-like structure with several rooms. An X marked a spot on one of the walls. A pile of round rocks was clearly drawn on the map.

"This looks like a treasure map," he whispered. "I'll bet that guy will flip when he discovers it's gone." Grant carefully folded the map and stuffed it inside his backpack for safekeeping.

The kids followed Mimi and Papa into the noisy, crowded airport. "Everyone get your passports out and please stay together," Papa said. "Brazilian customs officials are very particular, especially about electronics." He glanced around and sighed. "With this big crowd, it's going to take awhile."

Grant took a minute to scan the airport for the man on the plane. He recognized several passengers from their flight waiting by the luggage belt, but the man with the Panama hat was not among them. *Now where is he?* Grant thought.

As they waited for their luggage, Grant showed the map to Mimi and Papa. After hearing his story, they were concerned that the man may have lost something of value. They decided it couldn't hurt to stop at the lost luggage counter and inquire if anyone had asked about it.

The woman at the desk was busy on the phone when they approached. She spoke Portuguese into the phone cradled against her ear as she furiously tapped at her computer. She held up her index finger and motioned for them to wait.

Papa looked at his watch. Mimi patted his arm and suggested that Papa and the girls go ahead and sit with the luggage. She and Grant would wait at the counter. So they waited...and waited...and waited. When Mimi glanced at her watch again, she realized they had been waiting a full five minutes. It was obvious the woman's conversation would be a long one.

Mimi turned to Grant and shook her head. "I'm sorry," she said. "This looks like a lost cause." She patted his head. "I'm sure the man can get another copy of the paper if he wants it. See? It's been faxed recently," she said, pointing to the date and time on top of the page. Mimi thought it strange that there was no company name or fax number listed, but that happened sometimes. She smiled at Grant. "You can keep the map and look for clues with the girls while we're here," she said. "That should keep all of you busy while I do my research."

"Wow, this is so cool!" Grant cried. "Thanks, Mimi." He ran to the girls and waved the paper at them. "Look, a new mystery for us to solve!" he shouted. He held his hand up for a high-five, and the two girls joined his in a loud slap.

Rainy Rainforest

Outside, as the group stood at the curb waiting for a taxi to take them to their hotel, they noticed that the clouds overhead looked dark and foreboding. They were about to be treated to their first tropical rainstorm! A taxi van finally stopped, and the driver loaded their luggage in a big hurry. He pointed at the sky, mumbled something to Papa in Portuguese, and hustled them all into the car. They had barely pulled away from the curb when the first droplets of rain spattered on the roof of the van.

Everyone cringed as they gazed out the windows. Thunder crashed, and jagged bolts of lightning shrieked across the sky. The storm was all around them, and the kids were a little frightened.

"I don't think my dolls are enjoying this ride very much," Christina said shakily. She had

Savannah and Juliet tucked safely in the backpack next to her.

The driver fought the wind and rain while he tried to assure them they would get used to the sudden storms. "Rain, it comes every day during the rainy season," he said.

"And how long is that?" Papa asked as the van dipped and weaved yet again.

"A much long time," he said. "Usually, from November to April."

"Well that's just great," Papa said sarcastically.

Mimi tried to divert the kids' attention by giving them some information about the hotel where they would be staying. "Well, kids, our hotel here may seem a little different to you at first," she explained. "We'll be staying in what is called a *cabaña*. It's on the hotel grounds, but it's like having a private apartment. Ours will have a kitchen, a living room, double beds and a couch that folds down when you want to sleep." Mimi knew it would work out perfectly for them since Papa and Grant would bunk together and she and the girls would stay in the other *cabaña*. "Mr. Wahoobi, who owns the hotel, has assured me that each *cabaña* offers a stunning view of the rainforest."

Mimi tried her best to cheer up the kids who were still staring wide-eyed out the window. "Oh, and by the way, Mr. Wahoobi has a son who is just a few years older than you, Christina," she said. "Kim has offered to act as a tour guide for you kids. He said he'd show you the ropes while you're here."

That got Grant's attention. "Ropes?" he asked. "I was hoping he'd show us how to swing on vines instead. Then I can pretend to be Tarzan. **ahhh-AHAHAHAH-ahhhh!**" Grant beat on his chest as he gave the Tarzan call.

The group laughed, and everyone felt better.

By the time they arrived at their hotel, the rain had stopped as quickly as it had begun. All Christina wanted to do was get out of the taxi and kiss the ground. But it was all soggy, so she settled for the dry, safe haven of the hotel.

The Rainforest Hotel was truly a tropical paradise. Hundreds of beautiful flowers scented the air, and tall palm trees swayed in the balmy breezes. The main building looked like a giant glass pyramid. A lush, green mountain loomed behind it.

Mimi was awestruck by the beauty before her. She turned and spotted the *cabañas* nestled along the south side of the hotel. A spectacular view of the Amazon River and the rainforest completed the picture. "It's all so gorgeous!" she said, as she slipped her arm through Papa's.

Mr. Wahoobi hurried through the front door to welcome them. *"Boa tarde!* Welcome to Brazil!" He quickly introduced his son Kim to the group. Kim was almost six-feet tall with dark, curly hair. He flashed them a brilliant smile, and the kids took to him instantly. He wore tan cut-offs, a white linen shirt, and a small, silver cobra snake charm around his neck.

The adults shook hands and Mimi introduced the kids. "Mr. Wahoobi, I've already told the children that Kim has offered to take them on a rainforest tour," she said.

Mr. Wahoobi smiled at his son. "Kim is very familiar with the rainforest as he has lived here all of his life," he said. Mr. Wahoobi explained that his father and grandfather had been powerful leaders of an ancient Indian tribe that still lived in the rainforest.

"Obviously," Mr. Wahoobi said, "I did not share their desire for me to follow in their footsteps. But young Kim will make a splendid leader one day." He patted Kim on the shoulder. "He has a special way with animals, and he is extremely attuned to nature. The children will be completely safe with him."

Papa and Mimi thought so, too. There was a quiet strength about the boy, and everyone felt it. "What do you say, kids? Do you want to go exploring in the rainforest with Kim?" Mimi asked.

"Hooray!" they all shouted.

Grant was nearly bursting with excitement. "How about right now?" he pleaded.

"We'll plan a day for that," Papa said. "I promise."

"Sweet!" Grant exclaimed. "Kim, will you teach me to swing on a vine?"

"We shall see, Young Grant," Kim replied. With a quick smile for his father, and for his father's guests, Kim led them to their *cabañas*.

They walked right by the pair of binoculars following their every move.

Fabulous Rio

Soon after they were settled in, Mimi and Papa called a family meeting to make plans for the next day. It was a unanimous vote to visit Rio de Janeiro and take a boat ride along the Amazon River.

"Can we invite Kim to go along, too?" Grant asked. "I asked him earlier and he said he would like to if his dad says it's okay."

Mimi smiled. "It seems that you've made a fast friend."

"He's really cool, Mimi," Grant said. "And I like it when he calls me, 'Young Grant.' It makes me feel important."

"Well then, come along, Young Grant," Papa said, giving him a friendly pat on the back. "We men will go ask Mr. Wahoobi if Kim can join us

tomorrow for the day while the womenfolk make
camp." He winked at Mimi.

The next morning, Kim arrived shortly after
breakfast. He was honored that the family had
asked him to join them. Mimi came out of the
bedroom wearing a long tropical sundress. She
fussed over Kim as if he were a member of the
family. "Everyone calls us Mimi and Papa, so
don't feel that you need to do any different," she
said. She scurried around with a dishtowel,
wiping the counter. "Have you eaten, Kim? Did
you bring suntan lotion?"

"Mimi will fuss over you all day if you let her,"
Papa said. "Come on, kids, let's go!"

The taxi ride into Rio de Janeiro was short,
and much to Christina's delight, the sun was
shining with no hint of rain in sight.

Rio was bustling with people, and the taxi
had slowed to a crawl. "Can't we go any faster?"
said Grant.

"I think we'd better walk to the dock," said Papa. "It's just a few blocks. But we need to hustle to make the tour boat!"

Along the way, Christina spotted several different groups dressed in magnificent costumes. "Look at all those dancers," she said. "Their costumes are incredible! They're so shiny and colorful—I see mirrors, shiny silk, feathers, even coins!" She motioned toward a group of dancers with enormous headdresses. "How in the world do they keep those things on their heads?" Christina asked. "It gives me a headache just thinking about it!"

Kim explained that they were preparing for *Carnival.* "It is like one giant party held outside in the streets both day and night," he told them over the beat of the drums. "People practice these samba dances all year long and compete at *Carnival.*"

The group found themselves swept along with the swaying samba dancers as they moved toward the dock. The pounding beat of the samba band made them all walk with a bounce in their step. The kids giggled as they tried to mimic the complicated steps of the samba.

"Hey, look at me!" Grant shouted. "I'm the samba king!" He imitated the steps of the dance—quick, quick, slow. When he tried changing from one foot to the other to get the hip motion right, his feet got twisted and he tumbled head first into some bushes. **"WHOOOAAAA!"** Grant cried.

Christina and Sam helped him to his feet. "Come on, samba king," Christina said with a laugh. "Let's hurry and catch up with the others."

While Papa went into the shop to retrieve their tickets, Mimi sat fanning herself on a small bench outside. "I haven't had that much **strenuous** activity in a long time," she told the children with a smile. "I'll be more than ready for lunch."

The double-decker boat left promptly at noon. It coasted along the water in a zigzag pattern so people on both sides of the boat could see the wide variety of wildlife up close. The Amazon River was brown, and not at all the way Christina had pictured it. "It looks so...well...like chocolate," she said.

"Yummy, chocolate," Grant said, rubbing his stomach.

"The Amazon River is brown because the current is swift and carries the mud along with it." Kim explained. "It's the second longest river in the world!" Kim grabbed Grant's skinny shoulders. "It is over 4,000 miles long and up to 300 feet deep in places, so don't fall in, Young Grant!"

The boat turned and the rainforest loomed before them like a solid wall of green. The air was cooler near the trees, offering a refreshing break to the heat of the day. The kids laughed and pointed as a family of dolphins swam alongside the boat. They leaped out of the water, raced with the boat, then turned and did it again.

Several alligators soaked up the sun on the shore as the boat drew near. Some of the passengers videotaped them while others commented on how ferocious they looked.

"Look at those alligators!" Grant said. "They're awesome!"

"Actually, they are called caimans here in South America," Kim explained. "But they are members of the alligator family."

Grant spotted a man along the rail who looked familiar. He was peering at the caimans through binoculars. Grant cringed when he saw the long, jagged scar on his cheek, and the Panama hat on his head. He anxiously tugged on

Christina's shirt to get her attention. "Christina, look!" he cried. "It's the man from the plane!" But when she turned around, the man was gone.

Christina scanned the other passengers, but did not see anyone fitting Grant's description of the man. "Perhaps you just thought it was him, Grant," she said.

"I don't know..." he said. "Where did he go?"

Christina was distracted by all the caimans. "I don't think they like us being so close," she said. Just as the words came out of her mouth, a caiman opened his jaws wide, showing all of his yellow teeth, and then quickly snapped them shut.

"**EEK!**" Christina shrieked.

"Maybe he's hungry," Grant said.

"I think you have food on the brain," Mimi said, and ruffled Grant's blonde head.

Sam pointed as a few scarlet macaws circled right over the boat. "They're so red!" she cried.

"I could watch them all day," Mimi replied.

The horn tooted three times to signal lunch.

"Food at last!" Grant exclaimed.

The group headed for the stairs that led to the restaurant below. They claimed a long table by the window where they could take in the magnificent scenery. The buffet was full of succulent seafood and a wide variety of fresh fruit, including bananas, pineapples, and coconuts.

Mimi passed a plate of crab to Kim. "What do you and other children of the rainforest like to eat every day?"

Kim smiled. "Rice and fish are served at almost every meal," he told the group. "Most of the children here know nothing of foods such as breakfast cereal, burgers, French fries, or ice cream," he said.

Grant's face turned pale with shock, and they all laughed.

Kim showed Grant how to crack the crab leg shells to get to the meat inside. "And this is how you eat them," Papa said. He made loud slurping sounds as he sucked the meat out of his crab legs.

"Hey, let me try that!" said Grant. Before long, they were competing to see who could make the most noise.

The boat returned to the dock by midafternoon. The samba music was still going strong and the kids' heads bobbed up and down to the beat while they rode in the taxi through town. Soon they were all fast asleep.

They never saw the man in the Panama hat hail a taxi and follow them to their hotel.

Creepy Crawler

The group returned to the hotel tired, but happy. Grant was still excited about what they had seen that day. Kim's father had allowed him to spend the night, so the boys were going to bunk in the bedroom while Papa slept on the foldout couch. The girls had already gone off to the other *cabaña* with Mimi.

Papa motioned to the bedroom with his chin. "You boys get settled in," he said. "I'm going to go see to the girls, and then I'll be back."

The two boys washed up and brushed their teeth. They hopped into their beds, threw pillows at each other, and settled in for the night. Papa came back and warned them from the other room that it was time to knock off the noise. After a little more snickering and giggling, they fell asleep.

Suddenly, something woke Kim. He could hear strange gurgling sounds coming from the other side of the room, then, "Aaaa...Aaaa..."

"Young Grant, it is not playtime anymore," Kim said, his voice groggy with sleep. "*Boa noite.* It is late, and I am tired."

"H-e-l-l-l-p m-e-e-e," Grant whimpered more clearly this time.

Kim sat up, alert now. "What is it, Young Grant?"

Kim threw back the covers and switched on the small blue lamp on the nightstand beside his bed. The soft glow of light cast shadows on the walls. He saw Grant's shadow, and then noticed something moving on Grant's chest— something with big, furry legs!

It was like a horror movie, only worse because they were the characters this time! As Kim looked from the shadow of Grant to the real boy, his eyes grew wide. On his chest was the biggest brown tarantula Kim had ever seen!

Grant could not speak. His breaths were coming out in short puffs, and his fingers dug into the blanket.

Kim needed to get help, and fast. His new friend was in big, big trouble. Most spiders in this part of the world were extremely dangerous, and he didn't want to startle it. "It will be all right, Young Grant, but you must stay very still, and don't make any sudden moves," Kim said in a comforting voice.

Papa heard the commotion and burst into the room. His voice boomed. "I thought I told you two boys to..." He took one look at Kim's frantic expression and knew something was terribly wrong.

Papa saw the tarantula on Grant's chest and moved cautiously toward him. Grant was trembling now as the spider inched its way toward his face. Sweat beaded up on his forehead. His tear-filled blue eyes looked up at his grandfather.

Papa motioned with his big hand for Grant to stay still. "Don't move a muscle," he said calmly and quietly. "I'm here now, and I won't let anything happen to you."

Papa took off one of his sandals and crept slowly...slowly toward the bed. He hesitated for only a second as he pulled his arm back to deliver the blow. Before Grant could even blink, his grandfather swished the sandal over his chest, knocking the spider to the floor.

Papa snatched a small bag from the souvenir shop off the nightstand and shook it upside-down, spilling its contents. He never took his eyes off the spider, which lay stunned on the tile floor.

Papa gently nudged the spider into the bag with the tip of his sandal. He planned to turn it loose outside. He carefully folded the edges of the bag down, and temporarily trapped the spider inside.

Grant sprang from the bed with a high-pitched squeal. "Yuck! Blah! Ewwwww!" he cried, beating his hands across his chest as if the spider were still there. He threw his arms out wide. "Did you see the size of that thing? I may never sleep again!"

Grant couldn't calm down. His adrenalin had been flowing, and now that he was safe, he was all wound up.

Papa grabbed him in a big bear hug. He stretched out his other big arm, and enveloped Kim in his embrace as well.

"My tummy hurts," Grant whispered into Papa's ear.

His grandfather understood completely. "Mine does too, son. Mine, too," he said.

The overhead lights suddenly switched on. Mimi stood in the doorway with her arms folded across her chest, the insistent tapping of her slipper-clad toe echoing on the tile floor. "What in the world is going on in here, with you men making all this racket while the girls and I are trying to sleep?" she demanded. Papa let go of the boys and bent to pick up the brightly colored bag off the floor.

Mimi immediately recognized the label on the bag. "What have you got there, Papa?" she asked with smile.

He looked down at the bag that was holding the spider and tried to hide it behind his back. "Ah, nothing," he said innocently.

"Did you buy me a present?" Mimi persisted. "Is it the topaz pin I saw while we were in the souvenir shop this morning?"

Papa looked down at the bag. "No dear, it isn't."

"It *is* the topaz pin, isn't it?" she asked. "You're trying to surprise me, right? You're such a dear." Circling in on Papa, she inched closer to the bag. "I already know what it is, so you might as well give it to me," she said. Mimi swooped in and whisked the bag out of his hand before he could stop her.

She smiled and peeked inside. Her eyes grew wide as she let out a scream and tossed the bag back to Papa. "How could you do that to me?" she cried, her hand over her beating heart. "There's a monster spider in there!"

"You didn't give me a chance," Papa pleaded, as Mimi scampered back to her room.

He turned to the boys. "You two get on back to bed while I see this little monster back into the rainforest where he belongs. Then I'll go and explain everything to Mimi." He winked at the boys. "This spider just cost me a topaz pin." He left the room, quietly closing the door behind him.

The boys looked at each other and had the same idea at the same time. They scrambled for Kim's bed and jumped in, pulling the covers all the way up to their chins. "Let's leave the lights on," said Kim.

"Okay by me!" said Grant.

Grant suddenly remembered the treasure map and wanted to share it with his new friend. He had been thinking about it all day. He leaned over the side of the bed and scooped up his backpack from the corner by the nightstand. He carefully unfolded the treasure map and smoothed it out on the bed.

"Kim, take a look at this," Grant said. He hastily explained the story of how the man had dropped it on the plane, then had simply vanished when they looked for him later in the terminal.

He held his breath as he waited for Kim to look it over. He was hoping that the building was somewhere nearby and they could explore it.

"Hmm, this really is a mystery," Kim said. "I don't recognize this building." He handed the map back to Grant, whose eyelids were drooping. Kim knew that Grant had experienced quite a shock, and what he really needed now was some rest.

"Let us turn out the lights, Young Grant, and get some sleep," Kim suggested. "We can speak of finding treasure tomorrow."

As they fell asleep under the covers, neither of the boys saw a man move from the window outside their cabaña into the nearby shadows.

Monkey Business

Papa's heroics were the main topic at breakfast the next morning. He and Mimi had told the girls about the tarantula last night, and after Papa left, they had slept with the lights on, too!

Papa leaned back in his chair. He stretched and yawned at the same time, making a sound like a growling bear. He admitted that he hadn't slept well, either, after their little spider incident, and that he was still a little tired. He stirred cream into his coffee, then pointed his spoon at the boys. "These two were both fast asleep when I returned to the room," he said. "They really had a big scare last night and handled it very well. I give them both a lot of credit after what they'd been through."

Grant lowered his head and swallowed hard. "If Papa hadn't come along when he did," he sniffed, "I don't know what would have happened. Thanks, Papa."

"Hey, little partner," Papa said, as he lifted Grant's chin and winked at him. "Heck, I was just doin' my job protecting the herd," he said in his best cowboy voice.

"Spiders, yuck!" Christina chimed in, trying to liven things up. "You were pretty brave, Grant. If that had been me, they would've had to carry me and my dolls out on a stretcher."

Kim shook his head in agreement. "Your sister is right, Young Grant. You were very brave, indeed." He raised his juice glass in salute. "I know it was a terrible ordeal for you, but the spider was probably as scared as you were. They are a bit disturbing to look at, but they are necessary here in the rainforest," Kim continued. "They help keep the bug population down and..."

Christina held up her hand to interrupt. "Please, don't say another word about spiders. They give me the creeps." She plopped another berry on her cereal and glanced over at her grandparents. "Besides, the story Papa told me on our first day here about there being no spiders allowed at this hotel was working."

Everyone laughed, and by the time the meal had ended, spiders were forgotten.

"Can we go into the rainforest with Kim today? Paleeeeese?" Christina and Sam pleaded.

Mimi glanced at Kim, who nodded his head and smiled.

Papa merrily slapped his hand down on the table. "It's settled then," he said. "You kids run along and have fun. Mimi and I have to see about a topaz pin."

The kids could hardly wait to start their tour with Kim, and hurried to meet him in the lobby a half hour later. Christina loaded Grant's backpack with bottles of water, suntan lotion, and mosquito repellent. The treasure map was still tucked inside.

Kim guided them down a path carved through the jungle. He slashed at the thick undergrowth with his machete. Christina was more than a little nervous about that big blade, and flinched when he swung it against some vines. "That's some big knife!" Christina exclaimed, keeping her distance.

Kim wiped the sweat from his brow with the back of his hand. "Not to worry, Christina," he said. "I have used a machete practically my whole life." He chopped away some more vines. "It is necessary for getting through the jungle."

As the children stepped through the area Kim had carved out of the rainforest, they entered another world. Instantly, they were engulfed by the richness of the air, heavy with oxygen and humidity.

Christina was **captivated** by the sights and sounds of the rainforest. She knew no photograph could ever truly capture its beauty. Parrots squawked, and wild parakeets chirped. Because it had rained earlier, everything smelled fresh and clean. Droplets of rain clung to the flower petals, like glimmering, iridescent rainbows. Insects swarmed and darted into the multicolored flowers to taste their sweet nectar.

"Oh, it's so beautiful!" Sam said. "Kim, you are so lucky to be able to see all these incredible sights every day!"

"Yes I am," he said. "Things grows so quickly here that there is something new to see every day." Kim lightly touched a new tree shoot rising up on one side of the path. "In a few months it will grow big enough to cross the path and change the floor of the forest. When I come this way again, I will have to cut a new path that will take me through a different way, and I will see more new things."

They had walked a short way into the jungle when Christina had a thought. "Kim," she asked, "have you ever heard about the legend of the Lost Treasure of the Rainforest?"

"Yes," Kim said. "We studied about it in school. It is a fascinating story."

"Tell us!" Christina begged.

The other two kids joined in. "Tell! Tell!" they chanted.

Kim held up his hands. "Okay, okay!" he said with a laugh.

Christina looked around for a place to sit. Large rocks covered in soft green moss dotted the edge of the path. They looked safe enough, but she asked Kim to check for snakes and spiders just to be sure. The rock she sat on resembled the back of a giant turtle.

The minute the kids sat, a massive swarm of mosquitoes dive-bombed them. Christina whipped out her bug repellent spray. She doused the area with spray until the kids began coughing from the fumes. "Stop, already!" cried Grant.

"Okay," Christina replied. "That should do the trick!"

Kim began his story. "Many years ago, a sacred necklace encrusted with diamonds, emeralds, aquamarines, and amethysts was stolen. It had been presented to the chief of a large village as an offering for his daughter's hand in marriage by the young chief of a neighboring tribe," he said.

"That's a really big present!" Grant cried.

Kim nodded in agreement. "The chief was also given gemstones in all shapes and sizes as part of the offer. They rested on a bed of red silk and were encased in a beautiful metal chest.

"The chief placed the gemstones and the necklace upon a stone altar in the great temple during the wedding celebration," Kim continued. "As the festivities wore on into the night, three thieves posing as members of the young chief's tribe snuck into the temple and stole the necklace and the gemstones. They escaped into the rainforest where no one could find them."

Christina hugged herself and shivered. "With all the **nocturnal** animals roaming around at night, that wouldn't be my first choice," she said.

"According to the legend," Kim continued, "their escape plan failed when they were attacked."

"You mean like by natives with spears?" Grant asked hopefully.

"No," Kim said. "By a pack of howler monkeys."

Christina pulled her sunglasses down her nose and peered at Kim over the top of them. "You're making this up, right?"

"I assure you, I am not," Kim said. "The chief used howler monkeys to guard the village against would-be attackers. They were very loyal to him."

Grant leaped to his feet. "Yeah, monkeys rule!" he shouted.

Christina was getting frustrated. "Grant, stop acting like a little kid," she said.

"But I am a little kid," he reminded her, with a lopsided grin.

"Okay, you two," Sam said. "Stop arguing and let Kim continue the story."

"Well," Kim said. "The thieves dropped the necklace and ran toward the Amazon River to get away from the attacking monkeys. But the monkeys followed them."

Grant thought the whole thing was rather funny. "Wow, police monkeys!" he said with a giggle.

"The thieves jumped into the canoe they had left by the river's edge and tried to escape," Kim continued. "The monkeys swung along the trees and swooped down on the thieves, pelting them with coconuts and bananas. The thieves wrapped their arms around their heads, trying to protect themselves. The next thing they knew, their canoe tipped over. The man carrying the case with the gemstones was swept away by the Amazon River. The police later captured the other two thieves."

"What happened to him?" Christina asked.

"The police searched and searched," Kim said, "but never found the necklace or the thief with the gemstones. It was later discovered that the thieves were from Peru, so many people thought the missing thief may have returned there. But he was never seen or heard from again so no one was ever sure."

"Do you think the monkeys took the necklace?" Sam asked.

"Perhaps," Kim replied. "No one really knows. That is why the legend has lasted for over a century."

Christina looked wistful. "I'd like to think the monkeys hid it somewhere safe, and are waiting for the right person to come along and find it," she said.

Grant giggled. "I'd sure like to see a monkey wearing a necklace prancing around in the rainforest!"

"There are many versions of the story," Kim said. He stooped down and wiggled his finger near where a tiny hummingbird sipped nectar from a red passionflower. To the children's amazement, the hummingbird lit on his finger like a pet. A few minutes later, it flitted away.

The kids all stood mute and their mouths dropped open. "How did you do that?" Christina said in awe.

"Do what?" Kim asked with a mischievous smile.

Christina threw up her hands. "Oh, nothing. I suppose you have hummingbirds at your beck and call every day."

"Shhh!" warned Sam. "I want to hear the rest of the story."

The kids followed Kim as he walked down the path. "Some say there never was a sacred necklace or gemstones," he said. "They think it was just a mysterious story made up by a member of the tribe to be passed down from generation to generation so that others would look for the treasure."

"I'm going to find the sacred necklace and the gemstones," Grant insisted.

"I wish you well, Young Grant," Kim smiled. "But do not be too hopeful. Many before you have tried, but failed."

"Don't even get him started," Christina said. "The mere mention of a mystery gets Grant all goose-pimply."

Suddenly, they were interrupted by a loud, screeching noise. Christina, Sam, and Grant covered their ears. "What in the world is making all that racket?" Christina shouted.

Kim smiled. "It is a howler monkey," he told her. "He bids you welcome to his home."

Christina removed her hands from over her ears. "Well, I can see how it got its name. Are there other monkeys living here that don't make so much noise?"

"There are about 30 different kinds of monkeys living in the rainforest, but the howler monkey is the loudest. In fact, it is the loudest land animal in the rainforest, and can be heard up to three miles away," he explained.

Christina shaded her eyes with her hand as she tried to spot the monkey. "Maybe the poor little thing is hurt, but I can't see it," she said. She looked worried. "Should we go and look for it?"

"I assure you, he is in good health," Kim chuckled. "You would never find him anyway if he did not want you to. Howler monkeys make their homes very high in the trees."

"Have you ever seen one?" Christina asked.

"Sure," Kim said. "Every once in a while one will get hungry enough to come by the hotel and dig in the garbage cans for fruit. The last one I saw was about four feet tall and had a very long tail. It helps them swing from tree to tree."

Christina nudged her brother. "Just like you, right, Grant?"

He answered her by hopping around like a monkey, trying to imitate the screeching noise they had just heard. "**E·E·E, Ooh·Ooh·Ooh!**"

"Okay, okay," Kim laughed, as he watched Grant's antics. "They also have very long, powerful arms with five-fingered hands for gripping the branches."

Just then, the screeching began again, even louder this time, and the kids all looked up as a large blur swooped through the trees directly toward them.

"Duck!" yelled Christina, dropping to the ground as the monkey swung into a tree right above their heads. It looked down at Christina as if trying to tell her something. Then it dropped something at her feet, and swung off into the trees.

"Boy, that was close," Christina said, as she swiped the hair out of her eyes. "I've never seen anything like that before!" She glanced down at the ground and saw a small, folded piece of paper.

"Maybe it's a clue!" Grant offered.

Christina unfolded the paper carefully. The others edged in to get a closer look. She stared at Grant in astonishment. "It is a clue!" she cried. "It says:

If you want to
find the missing treasure,
follow the rainbow.

Christina glanced in the direction the monkey had come from, and wondered who had sent the note. It was obvious it wasn't the monkey. She looked to the sky and gasped. A spectacular rainbow arched high above the lake, ending in an unknown place somewhere deep in the rainforest. Gorgeous hues of red, yellow, and blue glistened against the overcast sky. Christina was sure she'd never seen anything as beautiful in her whole life.

"A rainbow is a sign of good luck," Kim said.

Christina believed in good luck and thought they would need a lot of it to solve this mystery. "It'll be good luck if it leads us to the missing treasure," Christina said.

As she and the others walked deeper into the rainforest, she looked all around and tried to shake off the feeling that they were all being watched.

Who Told the Witch Doctor?

Kim looked thoughtful. "Perhaps there is someone who can help you with this mystery," he said. "There is a very wise old man who lives just outside our village. Some say that he is more than 100 years old. He is called a shaman. You might call him a witch doctor."

"Witch doctor? Have you heard the witch doctor song?" Grant asked. He started to sing and bounce with the beat.

"I told the witch doctor I was in love with you.

And then, the witch doctor he told me what to do...

He said that
Ooo eee, ooo ah ah, ting tang
Walla walla, bing bang
Ooo eee, ooo ah ah, ting tang
Walla walla, bing bang—"

His sister interrupted. "Is he like a family doctor in America?" She knew Grant would just sing and sing if she didn't stop him.

"Not quite," Kim said. "He is like an American herbalist who uses plants to help heal people. His knowledge of plant medicines has been passed down to him over hundreds of years." He touched a dew-covered leaf on a nearby tree. "Here in the rainforest, one plant species per day is being destroyed by man's ravenous appetite for progress. He fears there will not be anything left for him to pass down to other generations."

When they arrived at Kim's village, the natives were busy fishing, harvesting bananas and coconuts, or weaving baskets. They glanced up as the kids passed by, and many waved to Kim.

An older woman handed Grant a coconut. "Thank you," he said. Coarse fibers covered the hard shell. "It looks like a monkey head with coconut hair," Grant laughed.

Kim held one in his hands for the girls to see. "Coconuts have many uses here," he said. "The fibers from coconut husks are used to make mats, mattresses, and rope. Coconut shells are used as dishes, like cups, or bowls."

Grant shook his coconut and was surprised when something sloshed around. "What's this jiggling inside?" he asked.

"It is coconut milk, Young Grant. I will show you how to drink it," Kim said. The old woman handed him a small paring knife, and Kim punctured a small hole in one of the "eyes." "Now you can drink from the shell, Young Grant."

Grant tipped his head back and took a swallow. The white, milky liquid ran down his chin and onto his shirt. He wiped his mouth on his arm. "Yum," said Grant.

"What does it taste like?" Sam asked.

"Well," Grant said as he ran his tongue over his lips. "It tastes like...coconut!"

The shaman sat on his haunches outside his hut. He wore a white turban around his head, and his skin was bronze and wrinkled from years in the sun. When the kids approached, he rose, but didn't seem surprised to see them. He and Kim locked wrists in a sign of greeting. He patted Grant on his head, then put his hands together and bowed his head at Christina and Sam.

"The shaman bids you welcome," Kim said.

The children mimicked the shaman and bowed in return. Christina could hardly contain her excitement. "Do you think he knows anything about the lost treasure?" she whispered to Kim.

"I will ask him," Kim said. He turned to the old man and spoke in their native language. "He says the legend is real," Kim explained. "At least that is what he believes."

Christina looked hopeful. "Has he ever seen the sacred necklace or gemstones?"

"No, but he has heard of them since he was a little boy," Kim answered.

Christina looked disappointed. She had hoped the shaman could shed more light on the legend.

Kim turned again to the shaman, and after a moment, translated for Christina. "The shaman has great powers of sight, and lately has had visions in which he has seen not only the treasure, but the one who will find it."

Christina stood up. "Who? Who will find it?" she asked, wide-eyed.

Kim posed the question to the shaman. The old man seemed to hesitate before answering him. When he did, his shoulders shook with laughter, and Christina was surprised when he gave her a wide, toothless smile.

Kim smiled, too. "He says that if he told you, you would not have any fun trying to solve the mystery yourselves."

The shaman's expression suddenly turned grim. He spoke to Kim in hushed tones. Kim's head snapped up and his eyes locked with Christina's. When they had finished speaking, he took her by the elbow and led her away from the others.

She held her breath in anticipation as Kim related the shaman's message to her. "He says there is one who will try to stand between you and the treasure you seek," he said. "He says that Young Grant holds the key to solving the mystery, and that we must all stick together in order to protect him."

Kim looked worried. "I already know that spider did not get into our room last night by accident," he said.

Christina was speechless. She was afraid that someone was really trying to hurt Grant.

"Come on, you two!" Grant hollered. "What's taking so long?"

Christina put her hand on Kim's arm. "We'll keep an eye on him," she said. "If it gets any more dangerous, I'll tell Mimi and Papa. But for now, let's just be very careful and see what happens."

Kim agreed, and they walked back to where Grant and Sam stood.

They never saw the man hiding in the bushes snap a picture of the four of them.

Pretty Piranha

"We should have stayed on the path," Kim warned. The forest was dense, and the fireball sun sunk low.

"Let's go a little further," Christina coaxed. "I'm trying to change direction in case someone's following us. See? There's another path."

She ran ahead. "Look, a lake!" She ran to the edge, slipped out of her shoes and socks, and prepared to dunk her toes in the water.

"Wait!" Kim cried.

Christina yanked her feet back. She spun and pointed her finger at his chest. "You scared the daylights out of me!"

"Look," Kim said, pointing to the water.

"What? All I see is a school of yellow fish waiting to make friends with us," Christina said.

"Make dinner out of us is more like it," Kim explained. "Those are piranhas, and they have razor-sharp teeth. They'll chow down on anything that gets into the water—birds, lizards, other fish, and girls who stick their toes in where they shouldn't."

Grant moved in to get a closer look. "Wow! They have a face like a bulldog," he said. "I didn't picture them being so big." He spread his arms wide. "Those must be a foot long! I'm glad we didn't try to take a dip in the lake." Grant stuck the toe of his shoe in the water, splashing it around to play a joke on his sister. "Help, Christina! They've got my foot! Awwww!"

Christina angrily pulled Grant away from the water.

"Wait a minute!" he yelled. "Come on, I was only playing."

"Pull a stunt like that again," his sister warned him, "and you might accidentally be left behind in the rainforest."

Grant gave her a sheepish grin and looked at Kim, who was trying not to laugh.

"You know, Young Grant," he said, "I think she may really mean that."

"Where do we go now?" Sam asked.

Kim pointed to the trees around them. "The brush here is too thick. We will have to go through the jungle by air."

Christina and Sam were stunned. "By air?" they said together.

"It is the safest way," Kim said, already climbing the exposed roots of a giant chicle tree.

Christina shrugged. "I'm up to it if you are," she said to Sam.

Grant was so excited he could hardly stand still. "All right!" He had waited all his life to swing from vines in a jungle. "Let's go!" he yelled.

"A short lesson first, Young Grant," Kim said. He tugged at the vine of a huge tree. "This vine is known as a *bauhinia guainensis,* or 'monkey ladder.' You can't do much swinging, but you can sway back and forth," he said. "Put your foot in those indentations. Then just hang on and swing."

"Aww, man. I wanted to swing through the trees like Tarzan," Grant pouted.

"In Tarzan movies, the vines were attached at the top, and free-swinging at the bottom," Kim explained. He pointed to the trunk of the tree. "In reality, those woody vines called *lianas* are not strong enough for a human to swing on. Only small animals can use them to travel through the trees."

Grant pulled on a vine to test it.

"Be cautious, Young Grant," Kim warned. "If you yank on a *liana,* something is going to happen."

"Oh yeah?" Grant asked, yanking on a random vine. "Like what?"

Kim smiled. "The rainforest's bug collection may rain down on you."

That did it for Christina. "Grant, stop this minute!"

"You mean like this?" Grant jerked on another vine to tease his sister, but it backfired when he saw

Christina coming at him full steam. She reached out to grab him, but he was too quick and swung away before she could snatch him.

"Wheeee! Look at me, I'm swinging!" Grant shouted.

"He's not watching where he's going!" Christina cupped her hands around her mouth and yelled. "Grant, look out for that, um..." **SMACK!** "...tree!"

The kids raced to where Grant fell. When they reached him, he was sitting under a tree laughing, his hair full of bugs.

"Hey, are you all right?" Christina asked, concerned.

"Are you kidding?" he smirked, handing a vine to Christina. "Do you want to try? Or don't you like having all those bugs in your hair, too?" he asked, wiggling his fingers under her chin.

"Too? What are you talking about?" Grant motioned at Christina's hair. She reached up and felt wiggly things. "Oh my gosh...oh my gosh!" she shrieked. She frantically ruffled her fingers through her hair. Bugs littered the jungle floor as she shook her head. "That does it!" she snarled at Grant. With fingers shaped into claws,

Christina chased after her brother, who darted in and out of trees trying to dodge her.

Sam laughed and signaled to Kim. "Why don't you go and save Grant from Christina," she said. "We'll never get out of here if you don't."

Soon the kids were on the move again. Kim took the lead, and moved from tree to tree with Grant right behind him. Christina and Sam followed them, holding on to vines attached to the trees at ground level.

The man following them had a hard time keeping up.

Poison Arrows

By the time they stopped to rest, Christina was in a bad mood. Sweat trickled down her forehead into her eyes, making them sting. The hot, humid air felt heavy, like someone standing on her chest. She feared another step would sap the last of her strength. She'd swatted so many mosquitoes her arms were tired. She frowned at the can of mosquito repellent. "It says it works in deep woods," she said, flipping the can over her shoulder. "Yeah, right."

Sam picked up the can. "Ah, but it doesn't say 'deep rainforest,'" she said with a laugh.

Christina scratched at the bites on her legs. "I've already seen about a gazillion spiders. Why don't they eat some of the mosquitoes?"

Kim smiled. "They do, actually, but the frogs get most of them. Close your eyes and listen. You can hear them talking to each other."

Christina closed her eyes and concentrated on the sounds of the forest. She heard squawks, buzzing, whistles, and shrieks. She could clearly hear the frogs ribbeting.

Christina heard a new sound and opened her eyes. It was Grant rustling around in the bushes. "Look at my brother. He's right at home in the jungle," she said, pointing. "All the creepy-crawly things he loves are right here."

Grant crawled on his hands and knees and shoved his head into some spiky bushes. "Oh, look at the neat red frog I found!" he yelled. He stooped down for a closer look. The curious frog looked right back at him with black, beady eyes. "Look at all those spots!" Grant shouted. He reached out his hand to catch it. "Maybe Mimi and Papa will let me keep him."

"Don't!" Kim grabbed Grant's wrist just before he grabbed the frog.

"Owww!" Grant jumped back with a wail, falling on his backside. "Gee, Kim, you hurt me," he said, rubbing his sore wrist.

Christina took a step forward just in case she had to come to her brother's rescue.

Kim smiled at her bravery. "It is all right, Christina," he said. "I was trying to protect him, but there wasn't time to say so." He helped Grant stand up. "In the future, Young Grant, please be careful of what you touch in the rainforest." He pointed at the little frog. "If I hadn't stopped you, you'd be in more pain than you could believe! That frog is called a *poison arrow*." He motioned the girls to move in to get a closer look. "These frogs are protected by their own skin and are extremely poisonous," Kim explained. "If a predator even licks that frog, it will get so sick it won't ever try to eat one again!

"That's how they got their name," he continued. "Their poison is still used today by Indians for the tips of their hunting arrows and blowgun darts."

"Just one more reason for us to watch our step in the rainforest," Christina sighed, looking around nervously. She'd read about the fierce pygmy natives who roamed the rainforest.

They followed another path for a while, then stopped for a moment to catch their breath. Christina looked up to see a Morpho butterfly as big as a saucer hovering right before her. Sunlight danced on its shimmering blue wings. The butterfly dipped, then gracefully flapped off toward the trees. "Did you guys see that?" she said.

"See what?" Grant asked.

"That beautiful butterfly." Her brother and the others just shrugged. Oh, so now they think I've been out in the sun too long, she thought. "It was right here," she explained. As she pointed to the spot, she noticed a small, folded piece of paper on the ground. "It's another clue!" she cried. The kids gathered around her as she read:

The treasure lies where the water grows high.

Grant stared at her. "Are you telling me that a butterfly just dropped a clue off for you on its way to the forest?"

Christina pulled her hair back. "That's what I'm telling you. So stop looking at me like I just grew two heads and help me figure out this clue."

Grant sat down on a rock and plucked at his clothes. "It's so hot and muggy. I wish I could take a shower," he complained. "A nice, cool waterfall would do right about now."

"That's it!" Christina shouted. "Where the water grows high!" She gave her brother a hug. "Grant, you're the best!"

"Huh?" he said.

Christina turned to Kim. "Is there a waterfall near here?"

Kim pointed to a dense mass of trees. "Right through there is a small stream. If we follow it back into the jungle, we will find the waterfall."

The kids zipped along on their mission. Soon they heard the deafening roar of water. "It must be just ahead!" Christina called out as she broke into a jog.

She ran into a clearing, and there it was!

The waterfall was breathtaking. Tumbling down from a rocky ledge, it fell nearly 20 feet in a rushing gush. Christina watched in awe as it tumbled over huge rocks that churned the water into the rainforest and a narrow ravine beyond. Suspended between the falls and the water below was another incredible rainbow!

Grant rushed to where a smaller stream of water poured over a rocky ledge. He stood right under the falls and pretended he was soaping himself down. "It's like taking a shower—only better because no one is yelling that I'm using too much water!" he shouted as he doused his head yet another time.

"Hey, save some of that for the rest of us," Sam hollered over the roar of the water.

While they waited their turn, Christina took the opportunity to ask Kim some questions about the disappearing rainforest.

"Why would anyone want to cut down the rainforest, anyway?" Christina asked. "It's so beautiful, and a perfect home for all the animals, plants and trees. I don't get it."

"It is all about progress," Kim replied sadly. "People have been chipping away at the rainforest for years, but now they have become even more aggressive. They cut the trees for lumber. They burn parts of the forest to enrich the soil for growing crops, such as coffee, sugar, and bananas. After a few years, the nutrients in the soil are gone and the land is of little use.

"The rainforest is a wondrous place," Kim continued. "I have lived here all my life and someday I will find a way to stop the destruction. It is my destiny as future leader of my tribe."

He looked so sad that Christina wanted to give him some encouragement. "Maybe when Mimi's book is published," she suggested, "it will help everyone understand the importance of protecting the rainforest and they'll try harder to find a better way to preserve it."

Kim smiled. "Well, it can't happen soon enough for me."

"Me, either," Christina said, stepping on a rock to reach the small waterfall now that Grant had finished his shower. **"WHOAAA!"** she cried as she slipped on the rock and plunged into the rushing water. Caught in the swift current, she was quickly swept downstream.

"Christina!" Sam screamed. "Oh my gosh, Kim, do something!"

Christina could hear them shouting her name, but couldn't answer as she struggled to keep her head above water. She frantically clawed at some vines dangling from the trees, but missed. She ended up doing a somersault and came up sputtering water and gasping for air. That's when she saw a huge boulder sticking up out of the water. She paddled as hard as she could to avoid it, but the current carried her straight for it. Christina banged her knee on the rock and howled in pain. She grabbed a vine lying in the stream, and held on until she could stand. **YEOWWW!** she bellowed. The huge knot on her knee hurt like crazy.

What do I do now? she thought. She remembered reading in a magazine that if you got lost, you should stay in one place and wait for rescuers to find you.

Christina waited and waited. Why isn't anyone coming? she thought. She decided to follow the stream back to Kim and the others. But she was so disoriented she didn't know which way to go.

All eyes in the forest, some not human, watched and waited.

Carved in Stone

"Well, I'm lost," Christina said with a sigh. The thick, green wall of the jungle surrounded her. "Kim! Grant! Sam!" she shouted. Lightning streaked across the sky, and thunder rumbled. Christina sat on a rock and rested her head on her arms. She could feel each individual muscle of her body ache. "I'll just close my eyes for a minute," she whispered. She felt herself drifting...drifting.

A shriek ripped through the trees! Christina leaped to her feet. "Ouch, my knee!" she cried. After a heart-stopping moment, Christina identified the screeching as a howler monkey. It swung down from the canopy of trees above her. She crouched and covered her head with her arms, bracing for an attack. When none came, she slowly uncovered her head to take a peek.

A young pygmy boy stood in front of her. Motionless, neither of them even blinked. He looked to be about Grant's age. What Christina noticed most about him was his huge brown eyes —and the blowgun in his hand! His expression was not threatening, but Christina wasn't taking any chances. She stood slowly and was about to bolt when the boy did the strangest thing—he held out his hand to her!

Surprisingly, Christina felt no fear and held out her hand. The boy gave her arm a tug like he wanted her to go somewhere. She hoped it was in the direction of the waterfall so she could find the others.

They walked for a while before Christina sat on a log to catch her breath. She was tired and ached all over. "Can't...can't go on," she said, breathing heavily.

The boy let go of her hand and walked ahead. Slowly, Christina got to her feet. "Okay, I'm coming," she called. He waited patiently for her, surprising her when he reached out to take her hand again.

Christina smiled. "Lead on, little friend," she said. The boy just grunted and tugged her along. Soon they reached the waterfall. Christina was disappointed that the others weren't waiting for her. She was so tired. "Grant! Kim! Sam!" she called out, but heard only the thrashing water. Christina gazed down at the boy. "So what now?" she asked.

In answer, the boy tugged her toward the falls. They stepped up to the wall of rocks where the waterfall tumbled down.

The rush of water reminded Christina how she'd gotten into this mess in the first place. She backed away from the waterfall. The boy seemed to understand and began to climb the rocks without her.

"Hey, where are you going?" she called. The boy turned around on a rock, and made a motion with his hand. He seemed to want her to follow him. But the rocky climb didn't look very safe, and she was already pretty banged up. "I'll just stay here," she said, pointing to the ground.

He grunted down at her and scampered further up the rocks. Curiosity got the best of her, so she decided to see what had him so excited. She carefully climbed from one rock to the next. Water rushed over her feet, and she slipped a few times. Looking up, she saw the boy climb over the ledge at the top. Carefully, she followed him, and before she knew it, she was crawling over the rocky ledge in front of the waterfall. "Little boy?" she called.

She spotted him as he dashed through the waterfall and disappeared.

"Hey, wait for me!" Christina inched herself against a wall of rock to avoid the falls. "Don't look down...don't look down," she chanted. Ducking her head, she followed him through an opening in a rocky wall. She had to squeeze to get through the tiny opening. As her eyes adjusted to the darkness, she saw nothing inside except the boy. He hopped up and down near a rocky ledge in the corner, almost out of her reach.

"Did you lose something up there, little boy?" Christina asked. She smiled at him. "Is that what you wanted? Someone to help you get it down?" She stood on her tiptoes and saw a bunch of small stones piled high in the corner. She tried to shove them away with her hand. The boy hopped on the ledge and began to dig with his hands, throwing dirt and pebbles in Christina's direction. "Hey, cut it out!" she

cried. She wiped her eyes and was just about to give up when she saw a small leather pouch nestled in a narrow crevice along the wall.

Her heart pounding with excitement, Christina pried it out of its hiding place. With shaky hands, she brushed the dirt off, and tugged it open. Inside was a stone tablet. Carved into the stone was the drawing of a building, much like the one on Grant's map. Next to the pile of rocks was a tiny circle of stones. "It's the sacred necklace! They're together!" she exclaimed. "Thank you," she whispered to the young boy. "I don't know why you led me to this clue, but wait until the others see this!"

The boy turned and fled through the opening. Christina crawled back through the waterfall looking for him, but he was gone. She didn't want to be stuck there by herself. Tucking the tablet into the waistband of her shorts, she carefully began to climb down.

As she secured her footing, she heard Grant cry out, "Christina, what in the world are you doing up there? We've been looking all over for you!" She nearly slipped on a rock in her excitement to get down and show them what she had found.

Grant, Kim, and Sam were anxiously waiting at the bottom for her. They were dirty, tired, hungry, and had Papa with them. He rushed toward her. "Christina!" He held her close, lifting her off her feet to carry her. "When they came back without you, well, your grandmother got scared."

"I'm tired of this jungle stuff," she whispered against his neck. "Let's go back to the hotel." She was asleep almost immediately.

The man in the bushes threw down his Panama hat and tore at his hair. The girl had slipped right through his fingers!

Beware!

The children sat in the comfort of Mimi's small kitchen, where she carefully tended Christina's cuts and scrapes. She gently probed at Christina's bruised knee, feeling for injuries.

"I'm good, thanks, Mimi." Christina smiled as she prepared to tell them her remarkable story.

"You say a young native boy led you to the cave?" Papa asked. He gave her a sideways glance. "You didn't hit your head on a rock and just imagine it all, did you?" he joked.

"Oh, Papa!" Mimi gave him a playful swat on the shoulder.

Christina gently laid the stone tablet on the table. "The little native boy led me right to it. It was amazing!"

"Let me see if I have this straight," said Grant, counting on his fingers. "You got clues delivered by a howler monkey, a butterfly, and then a pygmy native boy?"

Christina beamed. "Isn't it great?"

"It's creepy," her brother said.

Sam could hardly contain her excitement. "I believe someone is trying to help you find the lost treasure of the rainforest!"

A feast was held in honor of the visitors. Along with Mimi and Papa, the children shared in the festivities while the drums of the tribal dances echoed into the rainforest.

"Hey, watch me!" Grant shouted to his grandparents as he stomped his feet and chanted with the others around the bonfire.

Exhaustion finally took over, and Grant had to sit down for a moment at his grandparents' table.

He gulped down a glass of fresh coconut milk. Some of it dribbled down his chin, and he grabbed a folded napkin next to his plate. When he unfolded it, he realized it was not a napkin, but a note!

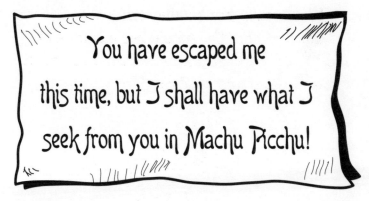

You have escaped me this time, but I shall have what I seek from you in Machu Picchu!

Grant nearly shot out of his seat as Papa laid his big hand on his shoulder. "What's got you so jumpy?"

"Aw, nothing," Grant said, crumpling the note so his grandfather wouldn't see it.

"It's time to call it a night," Papa said. "We're going to another country tomorrow— Peru! We have to be up early to catch the train to Machu Picchu!"

Grant's big blue eyes got even bigger! "But Machu Picchu is where..." he began, but stopped.

"Is where what?" Papa asked, surprised to see his grandson look so scared. "Grant, are you okay? You look a little pale."

"I'm just tired," Grant replied, "I think I'll go to bed now."

He knew he would not sleep this night!

Machu Picchu

"Picchu...Picchu!" the porter on the train cried out.

"It sounds like a sneeze when you say it real fast, like he's doing," Papa teased. "I almost said, 'Bless you.'"

When Christina didn't smile, Sam turned to Kim. "She's still upset. She thinks she failed because we had to leave Brazil with no treasure," she whispered.

Kim looked thoughtful. "What if we were looking in the wrong place? Maybe it wasn't in Brazil, but here in Peru!"

That got Grant's attention. He quickly told the others about the frightening note he had received last night.

Christina didn't like the fact that someone was threatening her brother, so her protective instincts took over. "I think we're getting close, maybe a little too close for Scarface. If it's a race to the treasure he wants, it's a race he'll get!" she whispered through gritted teeth.

"What's all the mumbling about back there?" Mimi asked. "Are you enjoying the trip?"

"Yes, ma'am," the girls said.

"Whooo hooo!" Grant chimed in.

The train slowly moved into the station, so there was no more time to talk about the treasure. With a few more bumps and lurches, the train came to a stop. The conductor tipped his hat as they stepped off.

"Oh Papa—look! It's breathtaking!" Mimi cried, as they got their first look at Machu Picchu. High atop a mountain ridge, it was an astounding complex built entirely of stone.

"Thank goodness we didn't decide to hike the Inca Trail to get here," Papa said, wiping his sweaty face with his bandanna.

Electronic guest information systems along the path with "You are Here" signs explained points of interest to the thousands of visitors who came to Machu Picchu each year. Papa pushed the button on the first one.

Sometimes called the 'Lost City of the Incas,' Machu Picchu, which means 'old peak', remained forgotten for over 400 years. The buildings were thought to have been built under the supervision of professional Incan architects. Built of granite blocks, the stones fit together perfectly without mortar. Although none of the blocks are the same size, the joints fit so tightly even the thinnest of blades can't be forced between them.

The group gazed at the stone structure as the narrator spoke. "This is the most amazing place I've ever been!" Mimi exclaimed, as they strolled to the next information system.

"Let me press the button this time," said Grant.

Thought to be a royal estate and religious retreat, the 200 buildings in Machu Picchu boasted temples, factories, water fountains, and even a jail.

Grant got all excited. "Oh, you know we've got to see the jail!"

"Yeah, sure, little brother," Christina said. "It'll be the first stop on our list." She glanced at Sam and giggled. "Not!"

Papa and Mimi had wandered to the next information system. The children still gazed at the buildings in wonder.

Kim was having the strangest sense of déjà vu, and something suddenly dawned on him. "Grant, let me see that map you've been carrying," he said. "And yours, too, Christina." Kim studied the maps and examined the building with the X on the wall. He compared it to the building in front of them.

The small pile of rocks in the corner of the map reminded Kim of the display of gemstones and necklaces that had caught his eye in the Machu Picchu souvenir shop window. "This is amazing," he said, holding the map out for the others to see. "I think the necklace and gemstones are here!"

"Why do you say that?" asked Sam.

"I think I figured out these maps." Kim said. He explained how he had seen gemstones and necklaces on display at the souvenir shop. "They sat in a random pile and I kept thinking that I had seen that display before," he said. "As you recall, neither the necklace nor gemstones were ever recovered, and the thieves were thought to be from Peru. What if the thief who was swept away in the river returned here?" He paused a moment to let his explanation sink in.

Christina looked hopeful. "Let's not waste another minute!" she cried. "We'll go to the souvenir shop and check out that display. If you're right, the treasure could be right in front of our noses!"

The kids stepped inside the crowded shop. Their eyes filled with amazement as they took in all the glimmering stones on display. Only Kim noticed that the clerk behind the counter was staring in Grant's direction. Her eyes met his briefly, then she focused her attention back on her customer.

"Hey, check out this cool caiman!" Grant cried as he made the animal's mouth open and close by pumping its tail.

His sister gave Sam a sideways glance. "Boys!" she said.

Christina rubbed her hands together in anticipation. "Okay, let's split up and look for clues," she said.

Kim was not certain they should separate after losing Christina in the rainforest yesterday. "I think we should stay together," he said anxiously.

Christina put her hands on her hips. "We're in a building, not the rainforest, silly," she pouted. "We're perfectly safe here."

"I know, but see that clerk over there?" Kim said, pointing to the register. "I don't know why, but she seemed to have an unusual amount of interest in Grant."

"She did?" Christina glanced over at the counter. The clerk was handing a man some change. "That grandmotherly looking woman? She's probably worried he'll break something," she said with a sigh.

"Plus, if we split up," Sam suggested, "we can cover more ground in a shorter amount of time."

It made sense to Kim, although he was still nervous about letting the kids out of his sight. "I agree, but please do not stray too far," he warned.

Grant laughed and pointed. "He sounds just like Mimi!" They all laughed when Kim narrowed his eyes at them.

As the kids started up the aisle, Kim ducked behind a pillar. He watched as the clerk motioned to someone with a slight jerk of her head.

Women in High Places

Christina was fascinated by the items on display in a glass case. She stopped for a moment to admire the sparkling gold chains encrusted with multi-colored gemstones. It was hard not to fantasize about the beautiful ancient necklace Kim had told them about. Last night, she had actually dreamed she had found it. She was so engrossed in her thoughts she didn't hear Sam speak to her at first.

"Earth to Christina. Hey, snap out of it!" Sam waved her fingers in front of Christina's face until she blinked a few times.

Christina was startled back to reality. "Hey, oh, what? I'm sorry," she apologized. "I was thinking about the lost treasure and I have a feeling we're close to something, but I can't quite put my finger on it."

Sam looked worried. "I'm sure you didn't hear a word I said, so I'll repeat it. I haven't seen Grant in quite a while, and I don't like it."

SMACK! "Ouch!" Grant rubbed his head. He had stooped down to look inside a display case, and when he stood up, he bumped his head on a man's elbow. He was still rubbing the sore spot when he turned to apologize. His mouth dropped open—it was the man with the jagged scar and Panama hat! He must have followed them here!

The man's grin was evil. "So we meet again, my little friend," he smirked. "You have something of mine, and I'm certain by the look on your face that you know what it is!"

The man reached out to grab Grant, but he ducked down quickly. "Give me the map, boy!"

"Help!" Grant yelled frantically as he struggled to keep his balance.

"Kidnapper!" someone yelled, pointing at the man. Everyone looked in Grant's direction.

"I'll deal with you later," the man threatened through clenched teeth as he backed away from Grant.

Security guards were still trying to get through the swarm of people when the kids made their move. Kim and Christina came from behind, hooked their arms through Grant's, and literally carried him away.

Sam came running at full speed. She shoved herself hard against the man in the Panama hat. He lost his balance and fell to the floor. The clerk came from behind the counter to block their way, but the kids just whizzed past her.

The clerk stood over the man with the jagged scar. "Go after them, you fool!" she shouted.

He swiped his hat from the floor, and started out after the children. They saw him coming and ran out the door and back to the hotel. Safe in Christina's room, they collapsed, panting from exhaustion.

"He was going to kidnap me!" huffed Grant, in between gasps of air.

"It is all right, Young Grant," Kim said, trying to catch his breath. He put a reassuring hand on his shoulder. "He will not have a chance to get you alone again, I promise."

Mimi startled them when she came out of the bedroom. "Hey kids, what's up?" she asked, taking in all the red, sweaty faces.

"Nothing!" they all said at once.

Mimi put her hands on her hips. "Uh, huh!"

Christina and Grant looked down at an imaginary something on the carpet. "Don't look in her eyes," Christina whispered to Grant. "She'll see right through us and know we're hiding something."

Mimi knew they were avoiding eye contact with her. "Well, I'm about to meet Papa down by the pool. Would any of you care to join us?" she asked.

The kids all looked at each other and answered at the same time. "No thanks, Mimi."

Christina stretched and yawned. "I'm kind of tired."

"Naw, Kim and I are going to stay here and watch movies," Grant chimed in.

Sam just shrugged, and fanned herself with a pamphlet she'd found lying on the table.

Mimi knew they were up to something, but she smiled and left the kids to themselves.

"Whew, that was close," said Christina. She looked up from her relaxing spot on the sofa. "Sam, what have you got there?" she asked curiously.

"Oh, this?" Sam answered, handing over the pamphlet.

Christina opened it and began reading about the history of Machu Picchu. "It says here that Machu Picchu was thought to have been inhabited by high priests. Hey, get this," she said as she motioned to the page. "Excavations of the site later revealed that of the 135 skeletons found here, 109 of them were women."

"Women?" Sam asked.

Christina's eyes grew wide. "No, it couldn't be that easy!" she said.

"What?" the kids asked in unison.

Christina pulled her hair away from her face. "Now, this is stretching the imagination a bit, but what if the thief who was swept away by the river was actually a woman?" she asked. "And, what if she made it back to Peru and sought refuge here in Machu Picchu? No one ever heard from her again, so it's possible she didn't want to be found."

Grant jumped out of his seat. "Oh my gosh! The treasure of the rainforest really, really could be here somewhere! This is soooo cool!" He started to say something to Kim about looking for more clues, but stopped. "Hey, wait a minute," Grant said with a scowl. "I thought I was going to be the one who solved this mystery!"

"Well, sometimes it takes a woman," Christina said, and laughed at her own quip. "A woman, get it?" she said, jabbing him lightly in the ribs. "You know, like the woman who everyone assumed was a man all these years?"

The man and woman listening outside their door snickered at her comment.

Dungeons and Dragons

The morning dawned bright and clear. Mimi and Papa were already dressed and ready to see more of the sights of Machu Picchu. The kids had slept late and were moving slowly. Grant and Sam wanted to see the jail, and Christina reluctantly said she'd go, too. Kim offered to take them if Mimi and Papa wanted to see something else.

"Bless you, my child," Papa said. "At the rate these kids are going, we'd have to wait all day for everyone to get ready. Come, Mimi, put on your straw hat and let's take in some of the sights."

The kids walked to the old jail among the ancient ruins after breakfast. Kim slowly led them into a narrow hallway. They were excited, and a little scared, as the light grew dimmer.

The group finally found their way to the stairs that led to the underground dungeon. It looked like no more than a big hole in the ground. "I don't know about this," Christina said with a shiver. "It's dark down there."

"Aw, don't be such a party-pooper," Grant said. He began singing the party-pooper song. "Every party needs a pooper, that's why we invited you, party pooper..."

Christina elbowed him in the ribs. "Cut it out, will you?"

Grant rubbed his side. "If you're not nice to me, I won't tell you that I have my camping flashlight in my backpack," he said, wiggling his eyebrows at her.

Christina spun around. "For once I could kiss you, dear brother!" She puckered up her lips and gave him a big, noisy kiss on the cheek.

"Yuck! I've been kissed by a girl!" Grant yelled, wiping his cheek off with his shirtsleeve. "And not only a girl, my own sister!"

Christina pursed her lips together and glared at him. "You're lucky I'm a girl or I'd..."

"Children, children," Sam interrupted, imitating her mother. "Can we please continue with our little adventure down into the dungeon?" She rubbed her arms as if she were cold. "If I have more time to think about it, I might not go at all."

Grant handed his flashlight to Kim, who moved down the stone steps ahead of them. The dungeon was chilly and the ancient cells smelled **putrid**. There was nothing left in any of them, except an eerie presence.

The kids felt their way along the stone walls. "Ouch!" Grant smacked his hand into something. In the dim light they saw stone rings attached to the wall where prisoners had been shackled.

"Wow! Ancient handcuffs!" Grant said with a nervous laugh.

"Can you imagine being left in here forever?" Christina said, and shivered at the thought.

Grant and Kim stared at the walls, fascinated by how perfectly the stones fit together. They backed up a little to get a better look. Grant accidentally bumped into Sam and shouted, "Yipe!"

Sam let out a small scream. "You just about scared me to death, you know that?" she said in a breathless voice.

"Sorry," Grant said. "That man with the scar has all of us creeped out."

Grant went back to stand next to Kim, who ran his hand along the wall in awe. "This place was built over 500 years ago, yet all of the stones still fit. It is amazing."

Grant leaned forward and peered closely at one stone in particular. "Except for that one," he pointed out.

Kim instantly became alert. "What did you say, Young Grant?" he asked excitedly. "Which one? Show me!"

"See? Right here." Grant tapped one of the stones in the middle of the wall. Sure enough, all of the others fit perfectly, but one seemed to be slightly off where the corners came together.

"Where is your map, Young Grant?" Kim asked. Grant yanked the map out of his pocket and handed it to Kim, who shined the flashlight on it, then on the wall.

Kim broke into a big smile. "I think you may have found something, Young Grant!" he cried.

The girls gathered around for a better look.

Grant could hardly contain his excitement. "What is it?"

Kim ran his finger along the edges of the stone. "I am not sure yet, but it may be the hiding place of the lost treasure of the rainforest!"

"Thanks, kids," said a raspy voice behind them. The group shielded their eyes from the bright flashlight as the man with the jagged scar moved into the room. "I thought I'd lost you for a minute there in the souvenir shop," he said.

He rubbed his hands together greedily and gave them a sinister smile. "I would have been searching all over Machu Picchu if I hadn't seen you come down here," he shrugged. "You have my map, and I couldn't get another."

He glanced around for a second. "Who would've thought the treasure would be hidden in a jail? How ironic!" He cackled with glee and gave the kids a look that chilled them to their bones. "So you kids thought you could outsmart me and take the treasure for yourselves, eh?"

In a flash, the man tried to snatch the map out of Grant's hands. Christina screamed.

A female voice interrupted them. "Well, well, well, isn't this a happy little reunion?"

Kim and Christina gasped as they recognized the clerk from the souvenir shop.

"Ah, I see you both remember me." She patted her hair into place. "Oh, dear, I'm afraid that just won't do," she sighed, and turned to the man with the Panama hat. "Stanley, would you please be kind enough to escort these lovely children into a cell so we can take our leave to find the treasure?" She stepped in front of Grant. "I'll take that map now," she said, and plucked it easily from his hand. "That's a good boy."

She looked at Christina and smiled. "You're right, it does take a woman. Stanley, if you don't mind? It smells dreadful down here," she said, holding a lace handkerchief to her nose.

"You heard the Dragon Lady, kids," the man said as he backed slowly toward the steps. He motioned to the kids with his flashlight. "Now, all of you get into that cell over there," he ordered. The kids were too scared to move. "Do what I tell you! Now!" he snarled.

Kim took a step toward him, but the man waved the flashlight menacingly. "Don't try to be a hero, son," he told him, "I'm not in the mood."

Jailhouse Rocks

"DON'T YOU DARE TOUCH THAT CHILD!" Papa's booming voice and the pounding of footsteps echoed through the jail. The startled man dropped his flashlight. He and Papa both struggled to retrieve it. During the chaos, the Dragon Lady tried to slip past the men and spun around right into the waiting hands of the police.

"Papa!" Christina shrieked, as she fell into his waiting arms. Soon Sam and Grant joined her, and they all cried as he held them. His own eyes were misty. "You know how Mimi worries when you're not where you're supposed to be," he said.

Grant suddenly remembered the treasure map and explained everything to Papa. He ran to the wall and showed him the odd-fitting stone.

"How did you kids figure it out?" Papa asked.

"Well, Kim suspected that the building on the map Grant found and the buildings here were the same," Christina explained. She went on to describe how the pile of rocks and necklace resembled the ones in the souvenir shop. "The clues were everywhere," she continued. "We just had to look for them."

Christina took the pamphlet out of her back pocket and showed it to Papa. "We read in here that most of the mummies they found here during an archaeological excavation had been women," she said. "We knew that the thieves were from Peru, so we just followed our hunch that maybe the thief who fell overboard with the gemstones was really a woman. She must have come here where she'd be safe, and hid the jewels." Christina shrugged her shoulders. "It made sense that a woman would be able to take refuge here in Machu Picchu without being noticed. Few people even knew it was here until it was rediscovered in 1911."

Police detective Perez smiled kindly at them. "Let's see what we have here." He took out his pocketknife and scraped the blade along the perimeter of the oddball stone. He plucked at it a few times with the tip of the knife and pulled it loose.

While everyone hovered around, he pulled out the stone and found a hollow chamber behind it. He reached inside and touched something metal. It felt too big and heavy to be lifted with one hand, so he reached in with both hands and carefully slid it along. They could hear metal scrape against stone as he slowly pulled the item from its ancient hiding place.

Papa held a flashlight on the opening as the detective pulled out a beautifully decorated metal chest. It was about six inches wide and six inches deep. Detective Perez held it up for everyone to see, then handed it to Papa.

"Is that it?" Christina asked. The necklace just had to be there. She crossed her fingers.

The detective stuck his hand back inside the wall and felt around. "Wait! There *is* something else in here!" He pulled out a worn leather pouch. He pulled it open and smiled. "Hold out your hand, Christina."

Christina squeezed her eyes shut as he poured the contents into her hand. "Please be the necklace, please be the necklace," she whispered. She opened her eyes as the sparkling necklace spilled out! Even in the dimly lit cavern, the brilliant stones shot sparks of color.

"It's the lost treasure of the rainforest!" she yelled triumphantly.

"Hooray!" they all cried.

The Dragon Lady and the man with the jagged scar strained against their handcuffs to get a look at the treasure.

"The Dragon Lady and her partner here are famous smugglers," Detective Perez told them. "They might have stolen a national treasure if you hadn't foiled their plan."

The man pointed his finger at them. "Yeah, and we would have gotten away with it, too, if not for you meddling kids!" he snarled.

The Dragon Lady patted his hand. "Now, Stanley, things don't always turn out the way we want them to."

"Aw, Mom..." he trailed off.

"Take them away!" Detective Perez commanded. The police ushered the couple up the stairs. Detective Perez turned to Papa and said, "I always love that part." He smiled at the children. "You're heroes!"

Papa hoisted the chest over his shoulder and immediately headed for the stairs. Christina held the glimmering necklace in her hand. Except for the rattling inside the chest, the small procession marched silently into the sunlight.

Glimmering Gemstones

The group and Detective Perez met in the circular tower called the Temple of the Sun. They were anxious to open the chest but waited for Mimi to arrive. She was as anxious as the rest of them to see what was inside!

Christina trembled with excitement. "Won't it be great if it really is the lost treasure of the rainforest?" she asked.

"Yeah," Papa said as he worked to pry open the lid. It was rusted shut. "I'm starting to wonder if it's sealed by magic or something." He looked up at the kids with a mischievous wink.

"I sure hope no ghosts fly out of there," Grant quipped.

The lid wouldn't budge, so Papa pulled out what looked like a pocketknife.

Detective Perez frowned. Typically, prying with a knife was not a safe task. The tip could easily skip or jump and the knife could end up cutting someone. That's why he hadn't offered his in the first place. "Perhaps we should wait..." he offered.

Papa put up his hand. "No need to be concerned, Detective. This is a special knife. I use it for prying open rusted feed boxes on the ranch."

He held it out for the detective's inspection. The sturdy blade on the knife was dull and slightly squared at the end, like a screwdriver.

Satisfied, the detective handed it back to Papa. "Okay, let's give it a try."

Papa wedged the tip of the blade under the lip of the chest and gently pried along its edges. Excited and curious, the kids crowded around, staring at the ancient metal chest.

Christina crossed her fingers on both hands and closed her eyes tightly. "It is the lost treasure! I can feel it!" she exclaimed.

"Stand back, kids," Papa cautioned. He waited until all four kids stepped back before he gave a mighty twist to the knife. The lid sprung open!

Christina, Grant, Kim, and Sam rushed forward as he carefully lifted the lid. Staring into the chest, they all sighed with disappointment. The chest was filled with ordinary-looking rocks of all different sizes.

Grant picked one up. It shone a bit where the edges were chipped, but it was still just a rock. "Oh man!" he groaned, as he tossed it back in.

Papa looked up from the chest. "What's the matter?" he asked.

Grant shrugged. "I thought we'd found the lost treasure."

Papa grinned. "I think you did find the lost treasure!"

Grant pointed at the chest. "Those? They're just rocks," he said. "They don't sparkle like the ones in the souvenir shop."

Papa retrieved the stone Grant had discarded and turned it back and forth a few times in the sunlight. "This is what gemstones look like when they come out of the earth," he explained. "Like rocks." Grant watched as the edges of the gemstone sparkled.

Christina picked up another rock from the chest. At first she couldn't get hers to shine. "What about mine?" she asked.

"Hold it up to the light, and turn it," Mimi suggested.

"Like this?" Christina replied. Holding a gemstone the size of a golf ball, she turned it this way and that.

"Now, look closely," Mimi said. "Wait for it. There!" she cried out. "You just might have an amethyst."

Christina could see purple sparks glint on the edges. "Is that really an amethyst?" she whispered.

"We won't really know until the authorities test them," the detective said. "But if I had to make a guess, I would say yes, it really is an amethyst."

Christina was **elated**. She grabbed Sam in a big bear hug. "I can't believe it!" the girls cried in unison.

Kim beamed at Christina. "I will go now and call my father so he can tell the shaman of your find!" He turned to walk out the door. "I don't think he'll be too surprised, though," he mumbled.

Rainforest Rewards

As Mimi, Papa, and the children pulled up in front of the Rainforest Hotel, their taxi driver tooted the horn. Mr. Wahoobi hurried through the front door and rushed forward to welcome his returning guests and his son. He embraced Kim and each of the children in turn. Then he gave a hearty handshake to Mimi and Papa. As soon as he had received their call about the discovery of the chest, he had gone to his village and informed the old shaman. "There is someone here who is most anxious to see all of you," he said excitedly.

They stepped into the coolness of the presidential suite. There, sitting on a high-backed chair that resembled a throne, sat the shaman. Papa carefully set the chest down on the round table beside him. "We had a family discussion and we've decided the treasure really belongs to you and your people," he said.

The shaman ran his hand over the top of the chest and sighed. Tears glistened in the old man's eyes. As he spoke, Mr. Wahoobi translated for him. "My people are in your debt for the return of the sacred necklace and the gemstones they thought lost to them," he explained. "He says he had many visions of a young girl who would help our tribe." He looked at Christina. "When you walked into our village, he knew you were the one," Mr. Wahoobi said.

The shaman spoke in his native tongue once more. Mr. Wahoobi translated as he spoke. "One of my ancestors was the young chief who brought these gemstones as an offering for the hand of the old chief's daughter so long ago."

Grant looked at the shaman and said, "But now, there will be no legend for your people to talk about."

"The legend of the Lost Treasure of the Rainforest," the shaman replied, "is not nearly as important to our people as the message to the outside world that the rainforest is truly the lost treasure!"

The shaman asked Kim to sit next to him for a moment. He spoke quietly to him, then presented him with the chest and necklace. Kim hugged the old man, then turned to Mimi, Papa, and the children. "He says he hopes I will follow my dreams of saving the rainforest one day."

The group applauded and cheered.

The shaman whispered something more to Kim, who burst out laughing. He looked at Christina. "The shaman hopes the clues he sent you aided you in your search."

"What?" she asked, remembering the howler monkey, the butterfly, and the pygmy native boy. "How did he do that?" she asked, bewildered.

"Ah, it is the magic of the rainforest!" Kim said.

"Wow! We solved a mystery and proved a legend to be true!" Grant shouted. "That's pretty cool!"

"And I got to help!" exclaimed Sam.

Grant wiggled his eyebrows. "So what's next? I'm ready for more adventure and excitement!"

Papa held up his big hand to silence him. "Can we go home now, please?" He leaned his head against Mimi's shoulder. "I've had just about as much vacation as I can stand."

Everyone laughed. They were ready to go home, too!

About the Author

Carole Marsh is an author and publisher who has written many works of fiction and non-fiction for young readers. She travels throughout the United States and around the world to research her books. In 1979 Carole Marsh was named Communicator of the Year for her corporate communications work with major national and international corporations.

Marsh is the founder and CEO of Gallopade International, established in 1979. Today, Gallopade International is widely recognized as a leading source of educational materials for every state and many countries. Marsh and Gallopade were recipients of the 2004 Teachers' Choice Award. Marsh has written more than 16 Carole Marsh Mysteries™. In 2007, she was named Georgia Author of the year. Years ago, her children, Michele and Michael, were the original characters in her mystery books. Today, they continue the Carole Marsh Books tradition by working at Gallopade. By adding grandchildren Grant and Christina as new mystery characters, she has continued the tradition for a third generation.

Ms. Marsh welcomes correspondence from her readers. You can e-mail her at carole@gallopade.com, visit the carolemarshmysteries.com website, or write to her in care of Gallopade International, P.O. Box 2779, Peachtree City, Georgia, 30269 USA.

Built-In Book Club

Talk About It!

1. Would you like to live in a place with a rainy season from November to April where it rains just about every day? Why or why not?

2. After Papa rescued Grant from the tarantula, Grant whispered, "My tummy hurts." Has your tummy ever hurt after something frightened you?

3. What do you think piranha fish eat for dinner?

4. What was your favorite creature in the rainforest? Why did you pick that one?

5. Would you like to explore the rainforest like the children did? Why or why not?

6. Where did you think the little pygmy boy was taking Christina?

7. How do you think the heavy stones to build Machu Picchu got up to the top of the mountain?

8. Christina says that geography seems alive to her after traveling with Mimi and Papa to many interesting places. Do you like to study geography? After reading this mystery, can you see why geography can be really cool?

9. If you hadn't learned what uncut gemstones look like from reading this story, what would you have thought they would look like? Would you have had the same reaction as Grant did when he saw them for the first time?

10. Who was your favorite character in the story? Why did you like that person so much?

Built-In Book Club

Bring it to Life!

1. Pretend to be in the rainforest. Take a group hike in your local forest. Close your eyes and listen to the sounds of the birds and animals you hear and try to identify them.

2. Make up a story about the rainforest and use your friends as characters.

3. Ask your teacher if you can study the animals of the rainforest. Call it "Amazing Animals!" Each book club member can choose one animal that lives in the rainforest. Learn how it lives and what it eats. Make a drawing of the animal and share it with the class.

4. Play samba music during your book club meeting and learn the steps! You can find instructions on the Internet.

5. Find pictures of rare butterflies from the rainforest. Some are tiny and some are as large as a saucer. Draw and color them.

6. Draw a map of the Amazon Basin. Name each country that borders it and show how the water runs into it.

7. Using the Internet, identify the many medicine plants. Print them out and paste them onto a poster board. Write each plant's medical use under each picture.

8. Create the colorful headdresses of *Carnival*. Use the Internet to look them up. Draw and cut poster board to make them. Paint them, and use lots of glitter glue to make them shine in the sun. Add feathers, too. Have a parade to show them off and a contest to see who has the best headdress.

Amazon

Rainforest Trivia

1. Rainforests used to cover 14 percent of the earth's land surface; now they only cover 6 percent.

2. More than half of the world's estimated 10 million species of plants, animals and insects live in the tropical rainforests.

3. The Amazon gets nine feet of rain every year!

4. More than 20 percent of the world's oxygen is produced in the Amazon Rainforest.

5. Over 500 mammals, 175 lizards and over 300 other reptile species, and one-third of the world's birds live in Amazonia.

6. It is estimated that about 30 million insect types can be found in the rainforest.

7. The Amazon covers 2.5 million miles, about the size of the United States of America west of the Mississippi River.

8. The name Amazon comes from the Greek myth of the Amazonas, powerful women warriors whose courage and war cries terrified their enemies.

9. The Amazon Rainforest is full of world records. It has the largest beetle, the *Titanus gigantus*, which is 20 centimeters long. The smallest monkey, the sagui, or pygmy marmoset, also lives in the rainforest. It grows to a length of only 15 centimeters and weighs only about 100 grams.

10. There are more fish species in the Amazon river system than in the entire Atlantic Ocean.

11. At least one-third of the planet's bird species live in the Amazon Rainforest.

Glossary

 captivate: to charm, fascinate, or hold the attention of

déjà vu: a feeling of having already experienced a situation that is happening now

 elated: very happy or proud

excavation: the act of digging a hole or cavity

machete: a large, heavy knife used as a weapon or to cut vegetation

 nocturnal: active at night

 putrid: foul-smelling; rotten

refuge: a safe or protected place to stay

repellent: something that repels, or drives away

sinister: threatening or suggesting harm or evil

snicker: to give a sly or silly laugh that is partly held back, showing scorn or ridicule

strenuous: needing much energy or effort

Would you like to be a character in a Carole Marsh Mystery?

If you would like to star in a Carole Marsh Mystery, fill out the form below and write a 25-word paragraph about why you think you would make a good character! Once you're done, ask your mom or dad to send this page to:

Carole Marsh Mysteries Fan Club
Gallopade International
P.O. Box 2779
Peachtree City, GA 30269

My name is:
I am a:____boy ___ girl   Age:_____
I live at: _____
City:_____ State:_____ Zip code:_____
My e-mail address: _____
My phone number is: _____

_____
_____
_____
_____
_____
_____
_____
_____
_____

Write your own Mystery!

M ake up a dramatic title!

Y ou can pick four real kid characters!

S elect a real place for the story's setting!

T ry writing your first draft!

E dit your first draft!

R ead your final draft aloud!

Y ou can add art, photos or illustrations!

Share your book with others and
send me a copy!

Visit the <u>carolemarshmysteries.com</u> website to:

- Join the Carole Marsh Mysteries™ Fan Club!

- Write a letter to Christina, Grant, Mimi, or Papa!

- Cast your vote for where the next mystery should take place!

- Find fascinating facts about the countries where the mysteries take place!

- Track your reading on an international map!

- Take the Fact or Fiction online quiz!

- Play the Around-the-World Scavenger Hunt computer game!

- Find out where the *Mystery Girl* is flying next!